Ali and the Magic Ball

by:
Wayne Edwards

Illustrated by:
Raya Golden

Eloquent Books
New York, New York

Ⓔ
Eloquent Books
New York, New York

Eloquent Books
An imprint of AEG Publishing Group
845 Third Avenue, 6th Floor - 6016
New York, NY 10022
www.EloquentBooks.com

ISBN: 978-1-60860-367-1

Printed in the United States of America
Book design by Wendy Arakawa

To David & Obi,

Thanks for all
the support.

Wayne–

It was three in the morning in Riyadh, the capital city of the far desert land of Saudi Arabia. There was a sandstorm brewing outside, and soon there would be dust flying everywhere. It was good the windows were closed, as the apartment would have been covered with it. The fog was becoming bad too. A little girl called Jill was fast asleep in bed, and her cat, Ali, was on the rug beside her as usual. The wind began to howl. Ali hated the wind. He got scared, but he managed to drop off to sleep, too.

Jill, who was from Britain, lived in the big city of Riyadh with her family. Her father worked in the local bank. She liked living in the country and enjoyed the exciting adventures, having many new things to explore. Ali was a fine grey Persian cat—fluffy with big bright green eyes. His beautiful tail was his asset, and he could curl it right around him just like a brush. He would swish it back and forth across Jill's face as a way of waking her up in the middle of the night. He would do that if she failed to respond to a kiss to wake her up. Jill rarely got angry; she loved him and was used to his routine.

Like all cats, he was a nocturnal creature,
and he liked to wander outside and explore the
rooftop. He would sit on the wall and look with
fascination in the distance at the city's tallest
tower. It fascinated him the way it reached up
high in the sky, and it was his dream to fly over it.

If Jill was too sleepy and he could not wake her, her mother or father would be next in line for Ali's wake-up call, and they would let him out instead; this is what happened on this particular night. He had many cat toys to play with. Jill kept them all in his basket on top of the washing machine in the utility room.

She had recently bought him a new ball to play with.
It made a jingling noise too,
which he also liked very much.
He had not bothered to play with it yet though,
as he had so many other toys.

On this particular morning,
after Jill's mother had opened
the door and had gone back to bed,
Ali heard a little bird singing on the window
ledge outside of the utility room.

He jumped on top of his toy basket to see the little bird,
and one of his paws accidentally touched the ball.
It fell to the floor and made a clinking noise,
but did not break. Ali jumped down and
knocked it a little with his paw out of curiosity.

It made a jingling
noise and with that,
the ball started flashing.
There was a gust of smoke and then a magic
genie appeared. The genie said,
"Hello, Ali. This is a magic ball. Please make
two special wishes and they will be granted."

He jumped away from him in fright,
as he looked so very strange, but then the genie said,
"Do not be afraid; I am your friend."
Ali lay there, cowered down on all fours,
and then suddenly thought of something.
What about that dream now,
of jumping over the high tower?

Now was his chance, maybe he should not be afraid,
as long as he returned home to his lovely little owner.
He made his mind up.
"I want to jump over that high tower, which I can see
from the roof top," he said.
As quick as lightning, he was riding on a magic carpet,
heading towards the tower.
He held on tight with his little paws firmly anchored.

Soon, he had approached the top of the
tall building. It truly was a fabulous sight to see the
entire city below, as he circulated around it.

The tower, with all its fabulous changing lights,
continually transformed itself
from one beautiful color into another.
This was against a backdrop of glorious
stars, which sparkled like gems in the sky.

Ali wished he could take a star home and give it to Jill. The city below resembled a space station. Many other high buildings towered into the sky like space rockets. He circulated around for a few minutes and then noticed something bright heading towards him in the distance. It was making a terrific noise and looked like a flying saucer, although he could not be sure yet because of the sandstorm.

If it were a flying saucer, would he be killed, or maybe captured and taken away into outer space? All of a sudden, his past cat life passed before him, as he began to realize that this could well be the end of it. As it got closer, he could see it was a flying saucer. Then he remembered his second magic wish. "Please take me down!" he exclaimed, and the magic carpet began to descend rapidly back down to Earth again. The genie had answered his command. With a big relief, he landed safely and he could see the flying saucer soaring through the sky above him.

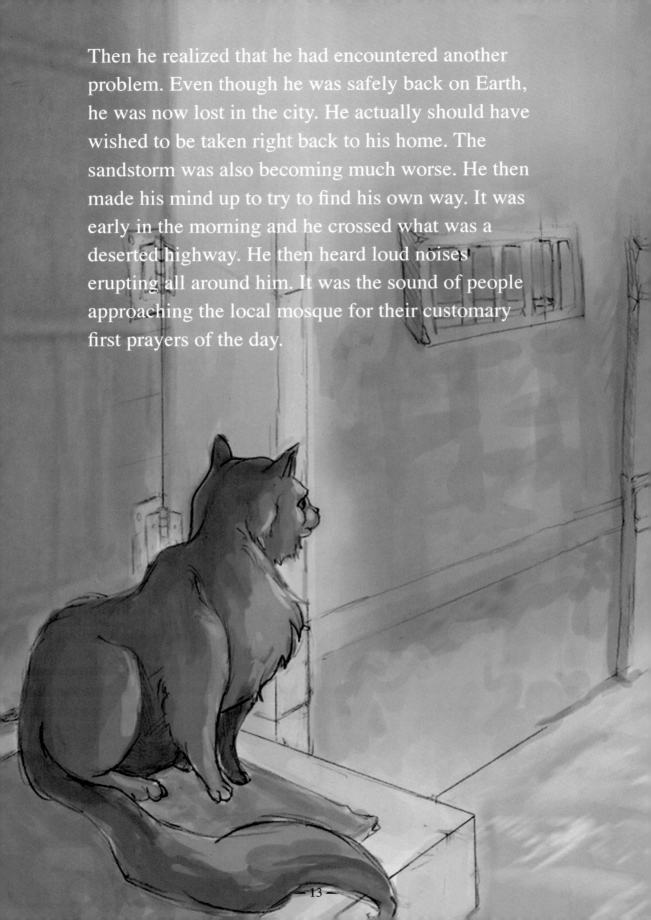

Then he realized that he had encountered another problem. Even though he was safely back on Earth, he was now lost in the city. He actually should have wished to be taken right back to his home. The sandstorm was also becoming much worse. He then made his mind up to try to find his own way. It was early in the morning and he crossed what was a deserted highway. He then heard loud noises erupting all around him. It was the sound of people approaching the local mosque for their customary first prayers of the day.

The city had suddenly come alive. He ran and huddled into a corner to hide; he was so scared. Even though Ali knew that the people of this land were good and honest, there would be a remote chance of someone taking him home with them; his bright green eyes were irresistible.He could then see that the people were starting to leave the building and go home again. He was safe. Nobody had seen him, and soon the streets of the city became deserted once again.

Then he ran as fast as his four little paws could take him in the direction west of the tower. His instinct told him that this was the way he had originally come. Faster he ran, whizzing around side streets, past garbage cans, and then he heard a faint little meow in the distance. A little stray cat was out there and was helping him.

Ali headed towards where the little meow seemed to come from. As the cat continued to meow, it seemed to be sounding as if it was becoming nearer, but he could not see anything because the fog had become so thick, and the sand was getting in his eyes.

He had to get home soon before it became even worse; otherwise, his chances of ever getting home would be over.

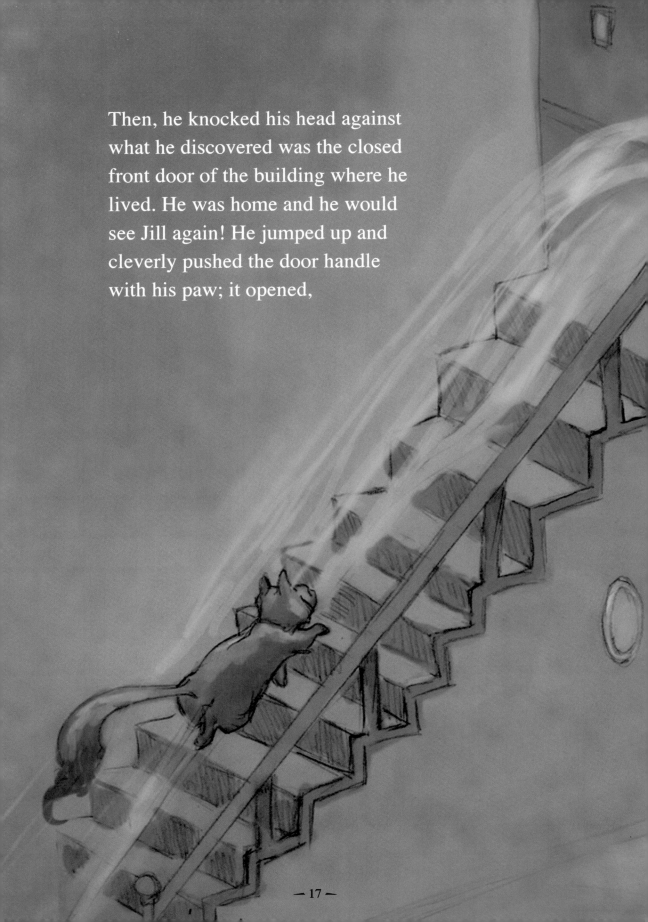

Then, he knocked his head against what he discovered was the closed front door of the building where he lived. He was home and he would see Jill again! He jumped up and cleverly pushed the door handle with his paw; it opened,

and he ran as fast as he could up the stairs
and onto Jill's bed. He started to shower
her face with kisses as never before.

"Good morning, Ali. Have you been out for your usual wander?" she asked.

He realized that he had only been dreaming.

It was time to wake up, yawn, and stretch.
One thing little Ali was sure about though
—he would not be going anywhere near that toy
basket for a long time to come.

After that awful dream, he decided to roll
over and go back to sleep. Jill did too,
before having to get ready to go to school. "Sweet
dreams Ali!" she said.

"Meow," he replied.
It was a silly idea anyway to want to go
to the top of that tower, he thought,
as he curled back to sleep.

The sand storm then finally began
to die down at last.

The End

LaVergne, TN USA
29 November 2009
1633LVUK00003B